The Messenger of Allah (peace be upon him) said, "*When a person dies his deeds come to an end except for three: Sadaqah Jariyah (a continuous charity), knowledge from which benefit is gained, or a righteous child who prays for him.*" (Muslim)

This book is purely inspirational and semi-fictional; it aims to open up the discussion between parent/guardian and children on deeds and actions that can be done for the benefit of a deceased parent, it is not an instructional book of Aqeedah.

Furthermore, the book only expresses the idea that we hope and pray that Baba's good deeds will lead him to Jannah, and that the rest of the family will meet him there one day, not that he is there already. Indeed, all matters of the unseen rest with Allah alone.

My Baba's House
A poem of hope for a child who has lost their father

First Published in 2022 by
THE ISLAMIC FOUNDATION

Distributed by
KUBE PUBLISHING LTD
Tel +44 (0)1530 249230
E-mail: info@kubepublishing.com
Website: www.kubepublishing.com

Author Dr Amani Mugasa
Illustrator Eman Salem
Book design Rebecca Wildman

A Cataloguing-in-Publication Data record for this book is available
from the British Library

ISBN 978-0-86037-861-7
eISBN 978-0-86037-866-2

Printed in China

My Baba's House

A poem of hope by Dr Amani Mugasa

"For Mohammad, may this book be a comfort for you until you find your Baba's beautiful house.

Umm Idris"

Dr Amani Mugasa

Illustrated by Eman Salem

Your Baba has been building
A beautiful house for you.
With Allah's help he made it,
There's just a little bit more to do.

Where is Baba's home?
It is there amongst the flowers.

But how did Baba make it?
It was made with Allah's powers.

With every blessed deed,
Your Baba became
a builder.
Every time he
smiled at you
The bricks turned
gold and silver.

And underneath the house
There are rivers
pure and **clean**.

Your Baba planted lots of trees,
The most **beautiful**
colour green.

How will you find your Baba's house?

It is **hidden** through Allah's gate.

The Angels will show you the way,
The path is **nice** and **straight**.

As you walk through the **garden**,
To your Baba's lofty home.
You will meet the **blessed** Prophets,
You **won't** have to walk alone.

On the trees are Allah's dates,
You can stop and have a taste.
But when you get to Baba's house
A feast of ripe fruits awaits.

As you **reach** your Baba's door,

You catch a **beautiful** smell.

Between the bricks
is perfume musk

And it's on your
skin as well!

And as the door is opened
You can see a cloak of silk.

stretching far beyond the house
To the rivers filled with milk.

You look up and see your Baba,
He lifts you with gentle hands.

And carries you above his head

To show you this new land.

Your heart is **full** of **happiness,**
You can't contain your **smile.**

As your Baba's
reunited,
with his **very**
special child.

How many **days** are left
Until this *blessed* day will come?
Allah knows which day it is,
He is the only **One**.

Your Baba is
waiting **patiently**
for the rest of
your **family** too.

Staring out of the window
Where Allah's **garden** is his view.

You can **decorate** your Baba's house with **roses** growing up the wall.

Allah will plant a **rose bush** with every **Adhaan** you call.

When you open the Qur'an
And read aloud Allah's words.

The house is filled with songs of praise
From Jannah's **beautiful** birds.

بِسْمِ اللهِ الرَّ

الْحَمْدُ لِلّٰهِ رَبِّ الْعَالَمِيْنَ

مَالِكِ يَوْمِ الدِّيْنِ

You decorate
your Baba's house

With pebbles made of pearls.

And when you become a grown up,
And with others share your money.

Flowing by your Baba's house
will be a river made of honey.

While your Baba **waits for you**
In the garden for a while.

A **present** of Dua for him
Will make your **Baba smile.**

I know the wait is difficult,
Patience we must learn.

And remember we
belong to Allah
And indeed, to Him
we return.